A HOME AGAIN

BY **Colleen Rowan Kosinski** · ILLUSTRATED BY **Valeria Docampo**

two lions

THERE IS NO REMEDY FOR LOVE BUT TO LOVE MORE.
—*Henry David Thoreau*

Published by Two Lions, New York

www.apub.com

Amazon, the Amazon logo, and Two Lions are trademarks of Amazon.com, Inc., or its affiliates.

ISBN-13: 9781542007207
ISBN-10: 1542007208

The illustrations were created with acrylic on paper and colored pencils.

Book design by Abby Dening
Printed in China
First Edition

1 3 5 7 9 10 8 6 4 2

For my children

—C. R. K.

With my last brick in place and
the final flower planted in my garden,
I was ready for my family to move in.
My timbers trembled in anticipation.

I soon delighted in the pitter-patter of a baby's tiny feet on my floors.
I swooned over the sweet scent of bread baking in my kitchen.

I treasured the sound of laughter echoing down my hall.

My family loved me. And I loved my family.

I was more than a house. I was a home. *Their* home.

My family grew and grew.
Each year the children were measured
with marks on my hall doorframe.

Inches grew to feet.
The soft pitter-patter turned into loud clomps.

Sometimes I got a bit banged up,
but my family always took care of me.

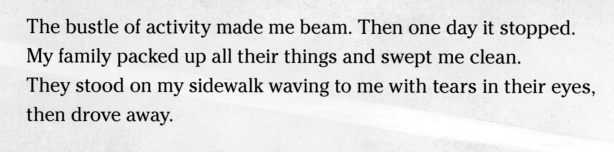

The bustle of activity made me beam. Then one day it stopped.
My family packed up all their things and swept me clean.
They stood on my sidewalk waving to me with tears in their eyes,
then drove away.

I was confused. They must be coming back.

Days went by.
People came to look at me.
They weren't my family;
I couldn't let them in.
When they walked up,
I'd shake my roof shingles to the ground.
I'd make my front steps creak,
my shutters dangle on their hinges.
Nobody ever stayed long enough
to open my front door.

Weeks passed, then months.
My family never returned.
Sorrow made my roof sag.
My garden turned brown and filled with weeds.
Tears ran down my windows, making them
smudgy and smeared.

Then a day came when two men walked up my driveway.
One sprinted to my garden, admiring the daisies that
had survived. The other bounded up my creaky steps
and pushed on my door.

I swelled it closed. He pushed even harder and . . .
it sprang open, rattling my rafters with surprise.

As the man walked across my floorboards,
I made them squeak.
"A few nails will fix this," he said cheerfully.

I forced cracks to splinter up my walls,
water to drip from my faucets.
He ran his fingers over the cracks
and turned the handles of my fixtures.
"Nothing some spackle and washers won't fix."

The other man joined him.
"This house is perfect."
My pipes warmed.

Then they left. My eaves sighed in sorrow. A few days passed.
They came back carrying paint and tools. I soaked the paint
deep into my walls so the color didn't take, but they kept trying.
It took three coats before I grew tired and let the paint stay.

They cleaned my windows and it felt so nice.
They hung beautiful paintings and silky drapes.
It looked so pretty I didn't have the heart to loosen
the nails and send everything crashing to the floor.

A big truck pulled up the driveway bringing furniture and boxes.
I wasn't sure I could be a home again.
My lights flickered at the thought.
The men tightened my light bulbs and kept unpacking.

One day they walked through
my front door carrying a baby.
She giggled, and my heart swelled.
Soon the pitter-patter of tiny feet
paraded across my floors.

Heavenly scents drifted from my kitchen.
And laughter echoed in my halls once more.
I loved this new family. And they loved me.

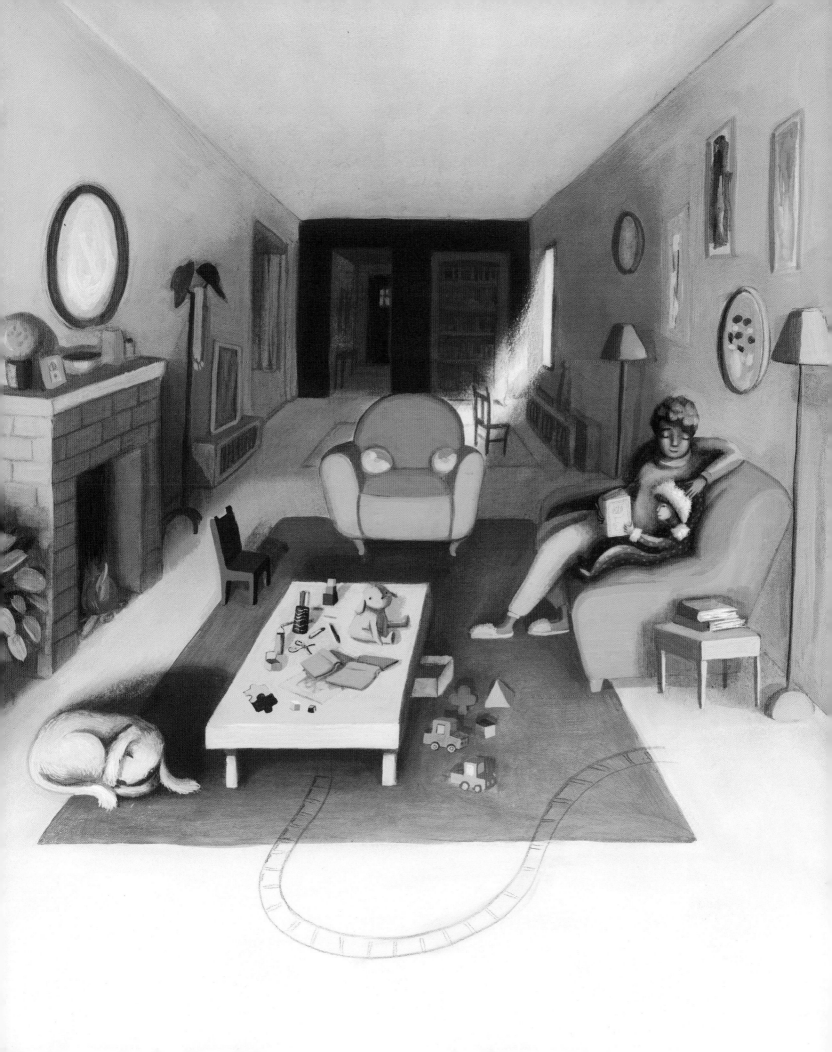

I was a home again.